# Secret PRINCESSES

# Brilliant Bake Off

ROSIE BANKS

Wishing Star Palace

# The Secret Princess Promise

"I promise that I will be kind and brave,

Using my magic to help and save,

Granting wishes and doing my best,

To make people smile and bring happiness."

# CONTENTS

## CHAPTER ONE
# A Sweet Treat

"Can we get some oranges, Mum?" Charlotte Williams asked her mother as they strolled through the bustling market hand in hand. Charlotte thought the stalls looked like rainbows, their wooden crates displaying brightly coloured fruits and vegetables – from glossy purple aubergines to ruby-red cherries.

"Of course," said her mum, handing
Charlotte a bag. "Get lots and we can
make juice."

Tucking her brown curls
behind her ears, Charlotte
leaned over a crate of
oranges and looked for the
biggest, juiciest ones she
could find. She breathed
in their citrus scent.
"Mmm," she said. "They
smell like sunshine!"

Since moving to California from England, coming to the local market on Saturday morning had become a new tradition for Charlotte's family.

"Get a few peaches, too," said Charlotte's mum. "They look good."

Charlotte added some plump, fuzzy peaches to the bag.

Bored of shopping, Charlotte's six-year-old twin brothers were pretending that they were space knights, using cucumbers as laser swords.

"Give up now!" cried Liam, swinging a cucumber at his twin brother, Harvey.

"Never!" shouted Harvey, blocking the blow with another cucumber.

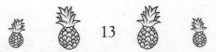

"Give me those right now or there'll be nothing left for our salad," Charlotte's dad said, interrupting the boys' duel.

"Aw, Dad," complained Harvey, reluctantly handing his father the cucumber. "You're no fun."

"Really?" said dad, raising an eyebrow playfully. "So I guess you don't want to help me make tacos for dinner tonight?"

"Tacos?" said Liam, his face lighting up. "Yum!"

"If you boys find me some avocadoes, we can make guacamole too," said Charlotte's dad, rubbing Harvey's short, curly hair affectionately.

When the twins returned, each holding

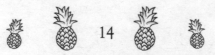

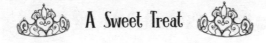 

a knobbly green avocado, Dad paid the farmer for their shopping.

"I think we all deserve a treat," Dad said.

Charlotte grinned at her brothers, her brown eyes sparkling. This was the best part of coming to the market!

Dad led them over to a stall with a mouth-watering display of cakes and treats.

There were gooey brownies, big, chewy cookies and cupcakes topped with swirls of buttercream icing. "You can each choose something," he told the children.

It was hard to decide, but Charlotte finally settled on a brownie. The twins both picked chocolate-chip cookies.

"Anything for you, hon?" Charlotte's dad asked her mum.

"Could I have an English breakfast tea, please?" she replied. Charlotte's dad ordered a tea for himself, too.

Charlotte grinned to herself. Even though her family seemed more American all the time, some things hadn't changed – like her parents still drinking tea!

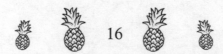

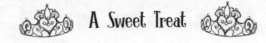 

As she walked through the market nibbling her brownie, Charlotte suddenly thought of Mia, her best friend who lived in England. Even though they now lived thousands of miles apart, Mia still sent Charlotte parcels of home-baked treats. For Charlotte's last birthday, Mia had baked Charlotte biscuits shaped like tiaras, stars and hearts. They tasted delicious, but the biscuits were more than just a yummy treat – they were a reminder of the amazing secret she and Mia shared. They were training to become Secret Princesses!

Shortly before Charlotte had moved to California, a family friend called Alice had given Mia and Charlotte necklaces

with matching half-heart pendants. Alice had explained that the girls both had the potential to become Secret Princesses, who could grant wishes using magic! Best of all, it meant that Charlotte and Mia could still see each other at Wishing Star Palace, a gorgeous castle in the clouds. Training to become a princess with Mia was the coolest thing that had ever happened to Charlotte.

Glancing down at her pendant, Charlotte gasped. It was glowing!

"I'm just going to have a look at that stall over there," Charlotte told her parents, who were tasting samples of honey.

Finishing the last bite of her brownie, she ducked behind some wooden crates.

No time would pass
here while she was
having a magical
adventure with Mia, so
Charlotte didn't need
to worry about her
parents missing her.
Holding her half-heart
pendant, Charlotte
whispered, "I wish
I could see Mia."

Golden light
streamed out of the
pendant, glowing
brighter and brighter
until it had completely

surrounded Charlotte. She felt the light whisking her away from the farmers' market.

*WHOOSH!*

A moment later, Charlotte landed in the marble entrance hall of Wishing Star Palace. Her denim dungarees and trainers had been magically transformed into a pale pink princess dress and sparkling ruby slippers. Charlotte patted her head, checking that there was a diamond tiara resting on top of her curls. But something was missing …

"Looking for someone?" asked Mia Thompson, grinning as she appeared out of thin air.

Mia was wearing a golden princess dress that matched her long blonde hair and sparkled like her blue eyes. Like Charlotte, she wore the glittering diamond tiara they had earned for completing the first stage of their princess training. On her feet were the ruby slippers they'd earned for finishing the second stage of their training.

"I've found her now," Charlotte said, running over to give her best friend a hug.

"You've been eating chocolate," Mia said, waggling her finger.

"How did you know?" Charlotte asked.

"Magic," said Mia mysteriously.

"Really?" Charlotte asked, her eyes growing wide in amazement.

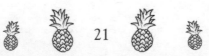

"No, silly," Mia said, giggling. "You've still got some around your mouth."

Charlotte laughed and rubbed the chocolate off. "I was at a market with my family," she explained. "You'd love it."

"I wonder where all the princesses are?" asked Mia.

They wandered through the ground floor, peeping into the throne room, the ballroom and the dining room. But the elegant rooms were all empty.

At the bottom of one of the palace's four towers, Charlotte could hear the faint sound of music and laughter coming from far above.

"They must be up there," Charlotte said.

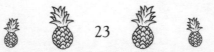

"It sounds like they're having a party!" Mia exclaimed.

"Well then," said Charlotte, holding out her hand to Mia with a smile. "What are we waiting for?"

## CHAPTER TWO

# A Starry Surprise

"We've never been up here before," panted Mia as they climbed up the twisting spiral staircase.

"There are lots of rooms we still haven't explored," Charlotte said. They'd visited the palace many times, but there was always a new place to discover!

As they reached the top of the stairs, a

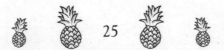

door opened. A princess holding a guitar beamed at them. She had cool red streaks in her strawberry blonde hair.

"Oh, hello! I was just coming to look for you," said Princess Alice. "I suddenly realised that you two have never been up to the Astronomy Tower before."

"We worked out where to go," said Mia.

"Of course you did," said Alice, giving both girls a hug. "Our trainee princesses are brave, kind AND clever!"

Back in the real world, Alice was a pop star. But Charlotte and Mia weren't star-struck because they had known Alice for a long time. She had been their babysitter when they were little, before she'd won a

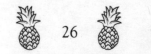

TV talent show and become famous.

"Come in," said Alice,
ushering them inside.
"We're having a party!"

The girls stepped
into a room with
a domed glass
ceiling. In the
middle of the
room, a huge,
gold telescope
pointed up at the sky.
A magical model of
the solar system floated
in mid-air, with gorgeous jewelled planets
orbiting a shining golden model of the sun.

The room was crowded with princesses chatting and sipping drinks.

"Wow!" said Charlotte, looking up at the stars twinkling overhead.

"It's awesome up here, isn't it?" said Alice.

"What are you celebrating?" asked Mia.

"It's a welcome home party," explained Alice. "One of our friends has been away

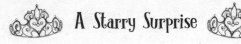 

from Wishing Star Palace for a whole year."

Charlotte suddenly noticed a banner stretching across the room. It read *Welcome Back, Princess Luna!* "Let me guess," she said. "Is her name Luna?"

"Yes," Alice replied, squeezing the girls' shoulders fondly. "And she can't wait to meet you!"

Alice led Mia and Charlotte over to a princess in a pearly white gown. Her dark hair was cropped short in a pixie cut and she wore a necklace with a pendant shaped like a crescent moon.

"Luna," said Alice, placing her hand gently on Luna's shoulder. "Can I introduce you to Mia and Charlotte?"

Luna's brown eyes widened in delight. "The new trainees!" she cried. "I've heard so much about you."

Mia blushed and smiled shyly. "It's really nice to meet you," she said politely.

"I love your pendant," said Charlotte.

A Secret Princess's pendant showed her special talent, which was why Alice's necklace had a musical note. Mia and Charlotte's half-heart pendants were very unusual – they showed that the girls had a gift for friendship, which was why they always worked as a pair.

Luna touched her necklace and smiled. "It's shaped like a moon because I'm an astrophysicist."

Charlotte's brow wrinkled in confusion. "An astro-what?"

"I'm a scientist who studies the universe," Luna explained.

"Luna knows everything there is to know about the stars and planets," said Alice. "Now if you'll excuse me, I promised Luna I'd play my new song for her."

"Why haven't you been here for so long?" Mia asked Luna, as Alice strummed her guitar.

"I was training to become an astronaut," said Luna. "I was so busy I had to take a break from my princess duties."

"A real, live astronaut?" asked Charlotte, staring at Luna in amazement. If her brothers knew she had met an astronaut they would be so jealous!

"A real, live astronaut," Luna confirmed, with a wink.

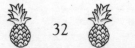

"That is so cool!" Mia said.

"I know," said Luna, grinning. "It's almost as cool as being a Secret Princess!"

"Nothing's cooler than that," Charlotte said quickly. They all nodded in agreement.

"I've wanted to be an astronaut ever since I was little," said Luna. "But it was hard to be away from my princess friends for so long."

Charlotte felt a pang of sympathy, imagining how sad she'd be if she couldn't see Mia for a whole year!

"Speaking of my princess friends," said Luna, gazing around the room, "where are Sylvie and Sophie? I haven't seen Kiko yet, either."

Charlotte and Mia exchanged worried looks. They dreaded telling Luna what had happened to her friends.

Charlotte took a deep breath. "They don't remember that they are Secret Princesses any more," she said.

"What do you mean?" asked Luna.

"Princess Poison tricked Princess Sophie into thinking she was showing her paintings at an art gallery called the Hexagon," explained Mia. "The portraits of Sophie, Sylvie, Kiko and Cara were cursed as soon as they were hung up."

Luna gasped. "That's awful!"

"The only way the curse can be broken is if they return to Wishing Star Palace," said

Charlotte. She sighed. "Unfortunately, they don't remember it exists."

"They don't even believe in magic any more," Mia added sadly.

"But Princess Cara is right over there," said Luna, pointing to a princess wearing a cool yellow dress and big hoop earrings.

Noticing them looking at her, Princess Cara, who was a fashion designer in the real world, came over. She hugged Mia and Charlotte. "Hey, girls."

"It's so good to see you back at the palace," said Mia.

"Well, it's all thanks to you two girls," said Cara. "Mia and Charlotte got me to believe in magic again," she told Luna.

"They convinced me to come back to
Wishing Star Palace, which broke the curse
on my portrait."

"It sounds like Princess Poison is more
dangerous than ever," Luna said sadly.

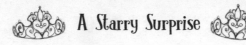 

Princess Poison had once been a Secret Princess, but she'd been banished from Wishing Star Palace for using wishes for herself instead of helping others. Now she spoiled wishes to become more powerful and was always trying to stop the Secret Princesses.

"We'll do everything we can to bring Sylvie, Kiko and Sophie back," Mia promised Luna.

"Oh, look!" said Luna. The moon at the tip of her wand was glowing. "Someone has a wish that needs granting! I'm a bit rusty, but I should resume my princess duties."

"No," said Mia. "You should stay here and enjoy your party."

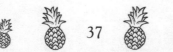

Charlotte nodded. "Can we do it? We're working towards getting our sapphire rings. We've already earned one sapphire, but if we grant another wish then we'll get another jewel."

When they'd granted four wishes – and earned four blue jewels – Mia and Charlotte would get their sapphire rings. The princesses' magic rings flashed when danger was near and could glow in the dark.

*I wish we had them now*, thought Charlotte, remembering all the trouble Princess Poison had caused on their last adventure.

"Of course you can go," said Luna. "Thank you."

The princesses wished Mia and Charlotte good luck as they headed out of the

Astronomy Tower. At the top of the stairs, Mia groaned. "We have to climb all the way down these stairs, then all the way another tower!"

"You're forgetting something," Charlotte said, tapping her foot. "We have magic ruby slippers!"

"Oh yeah!" Mia giggled. The girls clicked the heels of their ruby slippers together and said: "The Mirror Room!"

Magic swept them away to a small room, which was empty except for a huge oval-shaped mirror with a gold frame. In the mirror, Charlotte saw an image of the girl they needed to help. She had lots of beaded plaits in her hair, a pencil was tucked behind her ear and she was wearing an apron with a cupcake on the front.

Words appeared on the glass and Mia read them out loud:

"A wish needs granting, adventures await,
Call Ruby's name – don't hesitate!"

"Ruby!" Mia and Charlotte said together. The mirror swirled with light. As the girls touched the mirror, Charlotte felt herself being pulled into a tunnel of light. They were off to grant another wish!

## CHAPTER THREE
# The Cosy Café

Mia and Charlotte found themselves on a quiet high street. Glancing down, Charlotte saw that her princess dress had been magically transformed into skinny jeans and a fluffy jumper. Nobody had noticed the girls' sudden arrival, thanks to the way the magic worked.

"This is a cute little town," said Mia, who

was now wearing striped leggings and a tunic dress.

Looking down the street, Charlotte saw a newsagent, a butcher's shop, a bakery and a post office. A café with a cheerful red, green and yellow striped sign was in front of them.

"Something smells good," said Charlotte, sniffing the spicy aroma wafting out of the café. She rubbed off a patch of condensation to peer into the window and gasped. "I think Ruby's in there!"

Mia peeped inside and nodded. "It's definitely her. Come on – let's go in."

The girls entered the café, which was full of customers munching sandwiches and sipping hot drinks.

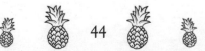

"Welcome to the Cosy Café," said the
girl from the mirror, smiling warmly. "I'm
Ruby." She handed the girls menus and
showed them to a table. "What can I get
for you?"

"What do you recommend?" asked Mia,
sitting down.

"Everything's delicious," said Ruby. "Of course I'm bound to say that – this is my grandparents' café."

"Can I have a hot chocolate and a slice of banana cake?" asked Mia.

"Great choice," said Ruby.

"I'll have that too," said Charlotte, handing Ruby back the menu.

As Ruby went behind the counter and gave their order to a man with long grey dreadlocks and a brightly coloured knitted hat, Charlotte suddenly realised something – they didn't have any money!

"How are we going to pay?" she whispered to Mia. Just then, she felt a tingle in her jeans' pocket. She reached her hand in and

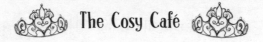
pulled out some money.

"Phew!" said Mia. "The Secret Princesses must be looking out for us in the Magic Mirror!"

While the girls waited for their food, another customer came into the café. She had wavy red hair and wore a pink vintage-style dress. It was Princess Sylvie!

The girls looked at each other in delight. If Sylvie was here then they could remind her about being a Secret Princess!

"Hi, Ruby! Hi, Frank!" she called, leaning over a glass counter.

"Hi, Sylvie," said Ruby. "Your usual tea?"

"Not today," said Sylvie. "Could I get a sandwich to take away, please?"

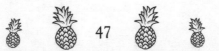

"Coming right up," said the man behind the counter with a lilting accent. "Did you have a busy morning in the bakery?"

Sylvie nodded. "I had orders for two wedding cakes and a birthday cake shaped like a hot-air balloon," she said. "I'm closing early today because I'm judging the village Bake Off," she said with a grin.

Charlotte looked out of

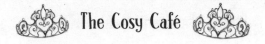 

the window at the bakery across the street. It had a pink and white striped awning and a sign that said *Sylvie's Bake Shoppe*. "The bakery across the street is Sylvie's!" she whispered to Mia.

Mia craned her neck so she could see out of the window. "It looks adorable!" she whispered back.

"Is your grandma going to enter the Bake Off?" Sylvie asked Ruby. "Her pineapple upside-down cake is legendary."

Ruby shook her head. "She's just not feeling up to it."

"Why don't you enter, then?" said Sylvie. "You're a great baker, too."

"Maybe," said Ruby, with a little shrug.

She headed over to a table, holding a tray loaded with sandwiches.

"Let's go and talk to Sylvie," Charlotte said to Mia. Maybe they could jog Sylvie's memory and get her to remember that she was a Secret Princess.

The girls went over to Sylvie, who was flicking through a newspaper while she waited for her sandwich. "Excuse me," said Mia. "We overheard what you were saying. What did your hot-air balloon cake look like?"

Sylvie smiled at them. "It had pink and lilac stripes made of icing."

"So it looked like the one you flew in at Wishing Star Palace," Charlotte said.

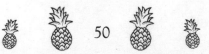

She desperately hoped Sylvie would remember the magical hot-air balloon.

"I'm sorry," Sylvie said kindly. "You must be mixing me up with someone else. I've never flown in a hot-air balloon. And I've definitely never been to somewhere called

Wishing Star Palace!"

"But you *have* been there," Mia insisted. "You make the most amazing magical cakes at the palace."

Sylvie laughed. "Some people say my red velvet cake is amazing," she said, "but it isn't magical."

"Here you are, Sylvie," said Ruby's grandpa, handing her a sandwich wrapped in white paper.

"Yum!" said Sylvie. "I'd better run. I've got to finish making an anniversary cake before the Bake Off starts." As she left the café, she called out, "I hope you'll enter the contest, Ruby. The deadline for entries is three o'clock."

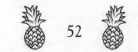

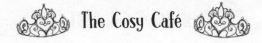 

Ruby brought the girls their hot chocolates and banana cake. Charlotte took a bite. The cake was moist and delicious.

"This is really good," she said. "Did you make it?"

Ruby smiled and nodded.

"So why aren't you entering the Bake Off?" Mia asked her.

"My grandma was going to enter but she's still not feeling well. She just had an operation on her hip," Ruby explained. "I really wish I could win the Bake Off for her, but I can't." She sighed. "Grandpa needs my help here at the café – it's too busy for him to manage on his own."

"Maybe we can help make your wish come true," said Mia.

"It's nice of you to offer," said Ruby. "But I don't see how you can help."

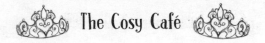 

"I'm Charlotte and this is Mia," said Charlotte. "What if we do the waitressing this afternoon? Then you can bake a cake!"

Ruby stared at the girls. "Would you really do that?"

"Of course," said Mia. "We used to play pretend at being waitresses all the time when we were little – it'll be fun to be the real thing!"

"Let me just check with my grandpa," said Ruby, hurrying behind the counter. A moment later, she rushed back. "He says it's fine!" she cried, sounding delighted. "Are you sure you want to do this?"

"Absolutely," said Charlotte, nodding. "Just tell us what to do!"

Ruby found aprons and notepads for Mia and Charlotte.

As Charlotte tied her apron around her waist, she glanced up at the clock on the café's wall. "You'd better get started on your cake," she told Ruby. "You don't want to miss the deadline!"

## CHAPTER FOUR

# A Pineapple Problem

"What kind of cake are you going to make?" Mia asked Ruby, as she showed them around the kitchen.

"I want to make a pineapple upside-down cake," Ruby told them. "It's my grandma's special recipe. But first I need to check whether we have a pineapple."

Mia and Charlotte followed Ruby into

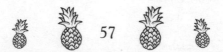

a small storeroom, crammed full of supplies. There were big jars of mayonnaise, huge bottles of ketchup and economy-sized packs of paper napkins.

"Oh good, we have one left," Ruby said, taking a pineapple off a shelf. "My grandma says that

using fresh pineapple instead of tinned
is what makes her upside-down cake taste
so good."

Back in the kitchen, Ruby started
gathering more ingredients. She took out
flour, butter, sugar and eggs.

Frank, Ruby's grandpa, smiled at the girls.
"Are my new waitresses ready to deliver
some orders?"

Mia and Charlotte grinned at each other.

Frank handed Mia a plate with a tuna
baguette. "Can you please take this to table
one – the lady with the baby?" Then he

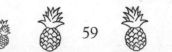

handed Charlotte two toasted sandwiches
oozing melted cheese. "Take these to table
three, please – the two ladies wearing
exercise gear. And when you're done, take
orders from tables two and four."

"No problem," said Charlotte.

She took the toasted
sandwiches over to
two ladies wearing
stretchy leggings and
trainers. "Here you
are," she said, setting
the toasties down with
a flourish.

"Oh, these look
delicious," exclaimed

one of the ladies.

"Good thing we've worked up an appetite this morning," said her friend, laughing.

"Let me know if you need anything else," Charlotte said.

Mia was waiting on a family with a little

boy, who was having a hard time making his mind up, so Charlotte went over to serve an old man sitting at table four.

"What can I get for you, sir?" Charlotte said.

"The usual – a pot of tea and a bacon roll," the man said, glancing up from his crossword puzzle.

"Coming right up!" Charlotte said, jotting down his order on her notepad.

"This is so fun!" Charlotte whispered to Mia as they headed back to the kitchen. Mia nodded in reply.

After giving the orders to Frank, they checked to see how Ruby was getting on with her cake. She was carefully measuring out her ingredients.

"Don't you need a recipe?" asked Mia.

Ruby shook her head. "My grandma and I have made it so many times that I know the recipe by heart."

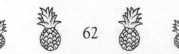

"Why haven't you added the pineapple?" asked Charlotte, noticing that the pineapple was still resting on the glass display counter.

"It doesn't go in yet," explained Ruby. "I'll put pineapple rings on the bottom of the cake tin, then pour the batter on top."

Frank picked up the prickly pineapple and held it up to his nose. "Ah," he said, inhaling deeply. "The scent of my island." He wiggled his eyebrows and made the girls giggle.

"My grandparents are from Jamaica," explained Ruby. "Pineapples grow there because it's warm."

"My wife and I set up our café over twenty years ago," Frank told them. "We serve food like jerk chicken and pineapple upside-down cake to remind us of home."

"My mum says that my grandparents had to work really hard to make the café a success," Ruby told the girls, her voice full of pride.

"It was worth it," Frank said, planting a kiss on top of his granddaughter's head.

"Hey," said Charlotte. "When is an apple not an apple?"

The others looked at her blankly.

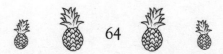

"When it's a *pineapple*," said Charlotte, grinning.

Mia and Ruby rolled their eyes, but Frank chuckled at Charlotte's joke. He had finished making the sandwiches for tables two and four, so Mia and Charlotte carried them out.

"One egg mayonnaise sandwich on white bread," Mia said, setting the sandwich down in front of the little boy.

"Thank you," said the boy's mum, smiling gratefully at Mia as she served her a prawn sandwich.

When Mia had given the boy's dad his chicken and avocado wrap, she nudged Charlotte. "Another customer came in

while we were in the kitchen," she said.
A person hidden behind a magazine was
sitting at the table closest to the counter.

Mia headed over to the table. "What
can I get you?" she asked the customer
pleasantly.

Startled, a girl with short, dark hair
lowered her magazine.

"Jinx!" cried Mia.

Charlotte whirled around and saw
Princess Poison's new trainee, Jinx. Princess
Poison was teaching her how to spoil wishes
and be cruel and spiteful – just like her.

Charlotte marched over to the table.
"Were you spying on us?" she demanded.

"She made me do it," Jinx blurted out.

She stood up so fast she knocked her chair over. Looking around wildly, she grabbed the pineapple that was sitting on the counter and ran out of the Cosy Café!

"Come back here!" shouted Charlotte, darting after her.

"We can't chase after Jinx," said Mia, pulling Charlotte back. "We've got customers to serve."

The girls returned to the kitchen, where Ruby was mixing up the cake batter. "Did I hear someone shouting?" she asked.

"It was me," admitted Charlotte.

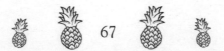

"Someone stole your pineapple."

"What?" said Ruby. "Why would anyone do that?"

"To prevent you from entering the Bake Off," said Mia.

"Where am I going to get another pineapple?" asked Ruby desperately. "The supermarket is too far away to walk there and Grandpa's too busy to drive me."

"Maybe the lady from the bakery might have one?" suggested Mia.

"Do you want us to go and check?" asked Charlotte.

"It's worth a try," said Ruby glumly.

Mia and Charlotte dashed out of the café and ran over to Sylvie's Bake Shoppe.

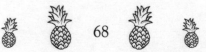

A heavenly aroma greeted them when they opened the door.

"Yum!" said Charlotte, eyeing the display case full of cupcakes topped with sprinkles. There was a scrumptious-looking red velvet cake with cream cheese frosting, a rich chocolate cake topped with strawberries, and a cake with layers all the different colours of the rainbow. Behind the display case were shelves of freshly baked bread, from thin baguettes to hearty wholemeal loaves.

"Hello," said Sylvie, looking up from the cake she was icing. "How can I help you?"

"Do you have any fresh pineapple?" asked Charlotte.

Sylvie shook her head. "I'm really sorry."

"That's OK," Mia told her. "We'll just have to use our wish necklaces."

"Your what?" asked Sylvie.

Mia held up her pendant. "Charlotte and I can use our necklaces to grant wishes."

"And so can you," said Charlotte, pointing to Sylvie's cupcake-shaped pendant. "Because you're a Secret Princess."

"Oh, I see," said Sylvie, winking at them. "Good thing our 'secret' is safe."

As the girls left the bakery, Mia sighed. "She doesn't believe us."

Charlotte linked arms with her. "Well, we just won't give up until she does," she said.

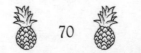

## CHAPTER FIVE

# Princess Poison Turns Up the Heat

Ruby looked up hopefully when Mia and Charlotte hurried into the kitchen, but her face fell when she saw that they were empty-handed.

"I may as well throw the batter out," she said sadly. "I can't make pineapple cake without pineapple!"

"No!" said Charlotte. "Let's check the storeroom again."

"Why?" asked Ruby. "There was only one pineapple."

"It's always good to double check," said Mia firmly, leading Ruby into the storeroom and shutting the door behind them.

As soon as they were all inside, Charlotte and Mia held their glowing pendants together, forming a perfect heart.

"I wish for a pineapple for Ruby," said Charlotte.

There was a flash of light and a pineapple magically appeared in Ruby's hands.

Ruby was so surprised she nearly dropped it! "What did you just do?" she asked.

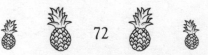

"We used our magic wish necklaces!" said Mia.

Ruby's brown eyes grew wide.

"We're training to become Secret Princesses," explained Charlotte. "We're here to help grant your wish. You wished you could win the Bake Off for your grandma, didn't you?"

"How did you know?" asked Ruby.

Mia smiled. "Magic! We can't make you win – but we can help you as much as we can. But you have to keep it a secret," she said.

"I feel like I'm in a fairy tale!" said Ruby. She pinched her arm. "Ouch!" she cried. "I guess I'm not dreaming!"

"Nope," said Charlotte, grinning. "You're wide awake."

"You'd better get back to your cake," said Mia, checking her watch. "There's not much time until the Bake Off starts."

"Look, Grandpa," said Ruby happily, returning to the kitchen. "There was another pineapple in the storeroom."

Ruby deftly sliced off the pineapple's prickly skin and chopped the yellow fruit into rings. She laid the pineapple rings on the bottom of the tin, then poured the batter on top.

"Looking good," said Frank, as Ruby slid the cake into the oven. He was busy chopping up red chilli peppers.

"What are you making?" Mia asked him.

"Caribbean fish curry," Frank said. "It's tonight's dinner special."

"I'd better start washing up," said Ruby.

"And we should clear some tables," said Charlotte.

As the girls removed plates from customers who had finished eating, the

  75

café door opened and a tall, thin woman strode in. She wore a tight green dress and spiky green high heels. Her hair was black, with an ice-blonde streak, and her green eyes glittered maliciously. Mia gasped. It was Princess Poison!

"What do you want?" demanded Charlotte, crossing her arms.

"Now, now," tutted Princess Poison,
sauntering over to a table and sitting down.
"Is that any way to treat a customer?" She
pretended to study a menu. "I'm ready to
order," she called loudly.

Reluctantly, the girls went over to her.
"Yes?" Mia said unenthusiastically.

"I'll have a green tea," said Princess
Poison. Smirking, she added, "And revenge
– served cold!"

"That's not on the menu," said Charlotte.

"Oh, yes, it is," said Princess Poison,
leaning forward. "I'm going to spoil Ruby's
silly little wish to get revenge on you
for breaking the spell I put on Princess
Cara's portrait."

"We won't let you do that," said Mia
defiantly.

"Oh, really?" said Princess Poison. "Well
get ready, because I'm about to turn up the
heat."

She stood up and pointed her wand over
the counter. Aiming at the oven, she hissed
a curse:

> **"Turn up the heat so the cake gets hot.
> It won't taste sweet and will burn a lot!"**

Green light shot from Princess Poison's
wand, but nobody in the café noticed what
was going on.

"Quick, Mia!" said Charlotte. "We need
to use another wish!"

"No," Mia said, shaking her head. "That's exactly what she wants us to do. We don't need to waste a wish to sort this out."

Mia walked into the kitchen and adjusted the oven's temperature dial. "Nice try, Princess Poison," she said, returning to her table. "But Ruby's cake isn't going to burn and we still have two wishes left."

"Oh dear," said Princess Poison, not sounding particularly concerned. "I really must try harder." She clicked her fingers. "Now, where's my green tea?"

Mia and Charlotte headed back into the kitchen and grudgingly prepared a pot of green tea for Princess Poison.

"How's the cake coming along, Ruby?"

Charlotte asked. Peering through the oven's glass door, she saw that the cake was rising nicely.

"It's almost ready to come out," Ruby said, drying a mixing bowl with a tea towel.

Charlotte carried the pot of tea out to Princess Poison, who was drumming her long nails impatiently against the table top.

"Finally!" she said. "I hope you aren't planning to become a waitress when you *fail* your Secret Princess training."

"That's not going to happen," Charlotte said, narrowing her eyes.

Just then, the kitchen timer rang.

"We'll see," said Princess Poison, raising an eyebrow and taking a sip of her tea.

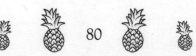

A loud cry came from the kitchen. Charlotte ran around the counter to see what had happened.

Ruby was holding the cake tin. "Oh, no!" she wailed.

"What's wrong?" asked Charlotte. The cake looked fine to her. It was a lovely golden brown colour, with little flecks of red in it.

"There are lots of funny red bits in it," Ruby said, sounding confused. "I don't know what they are, but they shouldn't be there."

  81

"Has anyone seen the chilli peppers I chopped up?" asked Frank, looking puzzled.

Mia and Charlotte exchanged horrified looks. They suddenly realised what Princess Poison's spell had really meant. When she said she was turning up the heat, she had put spicy chilli peppers in Ruby's cake!

They looked over the glass counter and saw Princess Poison gloating.

"Don't look so surprised," Princess Poison said. "I told you the cake would be hot." Draining her cup of green tea, she stood up. "Maybe you can enter it in a chilli contest instead," she called as she swept out of the Cosy Café, laughing meanly.

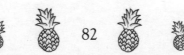

## CHAPTER SIX

# Upside-down Cake

"My cake is going to taste disgusting!" moaned Ruby, staring at it in dismay.

Mia and Charlotte looked at each other and nodded. It was time to use another princess wish!

"Don't worry," Mia told Ruby reassuringly. "We can sort this out."

Leading Ruby back into the storeroom,

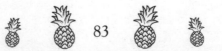

Mia and Charlotte put their pendants together again. "I wish there weren't any chilli peppers in Ruby's cake," said Mia.

There was a flash of light and suddenly all the red flecks in Ruby's cake were gone.

"Thanks so much!" Ruby said. Frowning, she asked, "Who was that lady, anyway?"

"Her name is Princess Poison," Charlotte explained. "She used to be a Secret Princess but now she uses bad magic to spoil wishes."

"The girl who stole the pineapple works for her," added Mia. "They don't want us to grant your wish."

Ruby looked alarmed, but Charlotte told her, "She's never stopped us before, and she's not going to start now."

"She sounds like an evil baddie from a fairy tale," Ruby said.

"But she's real – and really mean!" said Mia.

In the kitchen, Charlotte noticed that the cut-up chilli peppers were back on the chopping board. "Is this what you were looking for?" she asked, handing the chopping board to Ruby's grandpa.

"Silly me," said Frank, chuckling. "My wife says I'd lose my head if it wasn't connected to my shoulders."

As Mia and Charlotte held their breath and watched, Ruby carefully turned her cake out on to a cooling rack. It slid out of the tin perfectly. Now the pineapple rings

were at the top of the cake.

"Oh, now I get why it's called an upside-down cake," said Charlotte.

"Is it done?" asked Mia.

"Nearly," said Ruby. "I just need to add the finishing touch."

Standing on her tiptoes, she got a jar of glacé cherries down from a shelf. She popped a shiny red cherry in the middle of each pineapple ring. "The cherries add colour and extra sweetness," she explained.

"And they're ruby red, just like you!" said Frank, beaming at his granddaughter.

"Ta da!" said Ruby, holding up the finished cake. The cherries gleamed like jewels inside the yellow pineapple rings.

Juice from the pineapple had given the top of the cake a lovely golden glaze.

"It looks scrumptious!" said Mia.

Ruby checked the time. "I'd better get it to the Bake Off," she said, taking off her apron and hanging it up on a hook.

Mia and Charlotte left the kitchen to clear some more plates away. The lunchtime rush was over, and most of the customers had gone. Only the mum with the baby lingered, sipping a coffee as her daughter napped peacefully in her buggy.

"What if Princess Poison tries something else to ruin Ruby's wish?" Charlotte whispered to Mia as they stacked empty cups and dirty plates on a tray.

"I'm worried about that too," said Mia. "I really wish we could go to the Bake Off with Ruby, but we promised her we'd help out here in the café."

When they carried the tray of dirty dishes
back to the kitchen, Ruby had covered her
cake with plastic wrap and was ready to go.

"Good luck, Ruby," said Mia.

"I really hope you win," said Charlotte.

"Why don't you two go with her?" said
Frank, rolling up his sleeves and throwing a
tea towel over his shoulder.

"Don't you need us to be waitresses?"
asked Mia.

"It should be quiet in here until tea-time,"
said Frank. "I reckon I can handle any
customers on my own. Now hurry or you'll
miss the deadline!"

Mia and Charlotte grinned at each other.

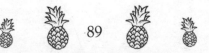

Whipping off their aprons, they followed
Ruby out of the kitchen.

"Where do we need to go?" Mia asked
Ruby as they walked briskly down the
high street.

"To the village green," said Ruby, who
was gripping her cake tightly.

As they neared the end of the high street,
Charlotte saw a grassy common up ahead.
There was an old church at one end of it,
and a cute duck pond at the other end.

A big white tent had been set up on the grass, and lots of people were streaming in, some holding cakes.

Looking up at the clock on the church's tower, Mia said, "We'd better get a move on – it's almost three o'clock!"

Speeding up, the girls hurried towards the tent. When they reached the entrance, a short, tubby man burst out of the tent and barged straight into Ruby. It was Hex, Princess Poison's servant!

"Whoa!" Ruby cried. The beautiful pineapple cake flew out of her hands, sailed through the air and fell on the ground. *SPLAT!*

Ruby covered her mouth in horror as she stared down at her cake, splattered all over the grass.

"You should be ashamed of yourself!" Charlotte told Hex angrily.

"Now it really is an upside-down cake!" he sniggered, stomping on Ruby's cake as he walked off.

"Last call for entries," said a voice inside the tent.

"We need to do something fast!" Mia said. The girls' pendants were glowing faintly now – there was only enough magic left for one more wish!

Mia and Charlotte pushed their half-heart pendants together. "I wish for Ruby's cake to go back to how it was," Charlotte said.

There was a flash of golden light and suddenly Ruby was holding her cake again. It looked just as good as it had before she'd dropped it.

"Quick – take it inside before Princess Poison can do anything else!" Charlotte urged Ruby.

They hurried into the tent and Ruby brought her cake over to a table heaving with delicious-looking cakes, pies and other baked goods.

"Thank goodness!" said Mia, sighing with relief as Ruby filled in an entry form. "That was a close call."

But Charlotte groaned as she noticed a girl with short, dark hair come into the tent. "Uh oh," she said. "Jinx is entering the contest, too."

Jinx's eyes darted around nervously as she walked over to the table holding a lopsided chocolate cake.

"Well, she's not going to win," said Mia. "My little sister can bake better than that."

"But your little sister can't do this," hissed a voice behind them.

Mia and Charlotte spun around to face Princess Poison.

"I'm going to make sure my trainee's cake is unbeatable!" Princess Poison said, pointing her wand at Jinx's pathetic-looking cake. Green light hit the cake, transforming it in a flash of magic.

Mia and Charlotte gaped at Jinx's new cake.

It was beautiful! It looked like a doll with long, dark hair and a billowing skirt made of cake. The skirt was lavishly decorated with layers of green icing that looked just like ruffles. Jinx's cake was a work of art!

Princess Poison hooked a long fingernail under Mia's pendant. "Oh dear," she said, pulling a fake sad face. "It's not glowing any more. No more wishes left to stop me." She threw back her head and let out a cruel laugh. "Victory will taste very sweet indeed!"

# CHAPTER SEVEN
# Cake Magic

When the judging began, Ruby came over to Mia and Charlotte. "Thanks so much for fixing my cake," she said.

"I bet the judges are going to love it," said Mia.

"There's a lot of competition," said Ruby. "There's one amazing cake that looks like a lady in a green gown!"

Mia and Charlotte exchanged looks. Jinx's cake did look amazing – but only because of Princess Poison's magic.

"Maybe it won't taste very good," said Mia, hopefully.

"Yeah," said Charlotte. "It will probably be really bitter." *Just like Princess Poison,* she added silently.

Charlotte glanced over at the table where Sylvie and two other judges were sampling all the contest entries. As they discussed the cakes, Sylvie waved her hands in the air and Charlotte caught a glimpse of magical blue light.

"Sylvie's ring is flashing," Charlotte murmured to Mia.

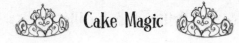
"It's warning her that Princess Poison is here," Mia replied.

Just then, Frank came into the tent, pushing a lady in a wheelchair. A man in a suit and a woman with plaits just like Ruby's were with them.

"You came!" squealed Ruby. She bent down and gave the woman in the wheelchair a kiss. "Mia, Charlotte, this is my grandma."

Then she went over and hugged the couple. "And these are my parents."

"When your grandpa called to tell me you were entering the Bake Off we knew we couldn't miss it," said Ruby's mum, smiling.

"Surprise!" said Frank.

Across the tent, Sylvie tapped the microphone a few times to check it was working. "Hello, everyone," she announced. "The cakes in this year's Bake Off were all wonderful." She patted her tummy. "My fellow judges and I have thoroughly enjoyed tasting them."

The audience chuckled.

"But we've narrowed our decision down to two cakes," Sylvie continued.

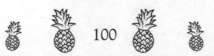

Another judge, a dark-haired man in black trousers and a white chef's shirt, stepped forward and held up Jinx's cake. "This gorgeous cake really impressed us with its technical expertise."

Princess Poison and Hex applauded loudly, though Jinx looked mortified.

"But looks aren't everything," said the third judge, a younger man with a ginger beard and glasses. "The second cake really has a terrific flavour and a lovely, moist texture." He held up Ruby's cake!

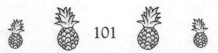

"Could the bakers who made these cakes come to the front please?" said Sylvie.

Ruby hurried up to the judges. Waving to her family, she beamed with excitement. Princess Poison shoved Jinx forward. Jinx stood at the front, fidgeting and staring down at her shoes.

"Your cake is very striking," the judge with the white shirt said to Jinx. "Where did you get your idea?"

"Um," Jinx said, shooting a nervous glance at Princess Poison. "I don't know."

Sylvie smiled at Jinx. "Could you tell us what ingredients make your cake special?"

"That will be tricky," Mia whispered to Charlotte. "She didn't even make it!"

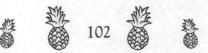

Jinx gulped. "M-mint?" she stammered.

"Mint?" said Sylvie, sounding surprised. "Really?"

"And, um, carrots and peanut butter!" Jinx added wildly.

The judges looked confused. "I thought it was a chocolate cake?" said the judge in the white shirt.

"Why don't you tell us how you made the icing ruffles," suggested the judge with the beard.

There was a long pause, then Jinx blurted out, "Magic!"

The audience laughed, assuming that she was joking. Jinx blushed as Princess Poison glowered at her.

Next, the judges turned to Ruby.

"Did you use any special ingredients in your cake?" the bearded judge asked her.

"I used fresh pineapple," she explained. "My grandma taught me that fresh

pineapple is the secret to a delicious upside-down cake."

"So this is a family recipe?" asked the judge in the chef's shirt.

Ruby nodded. "I've been baking it with my grandma ever since I was tiny," she said. "But it was my idea to add cherries on top."

As the judges huddled together to make their decision, Mia said to Charlotte, "I think Jinx messed up on purpose." She stuck her tongue out. "I mean, who would put mint, carrots and peanut butter in the same cake?"

But before Charlotte could ask why Jinx would have done that, there was an announcement.

"The judges have reached a decision," Sylvie said. "The winner of this year's Bake Off is Ruby, because her pineapple upside-down cake was made with lots of love!"

Ruby squealed as Sylvie presented her with a cupcake-shaped trophy. "This is for my grandma!" she said, holding her prize in the air. "She taught me everything I know about baking." Ruby ran over and handed her grandma the trophy.

As the audience cheered, Ruby's grandma clasped the prize to her heart. Tears of joy rolled down her wrinkled cheeks.

"We did it," said Charlotte happily to her best friend as they watched Ruby's family celebrating loudly.

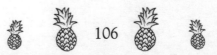

Breaking free from Frank's bear hug, Ruby ran over to Mia and Charlotte. "Thank you so much," she told them. "You really are my fairy godmothers."

Sylvie came over to congratulate Ruby, too. "I'm so glad you entered the contest," she told her.

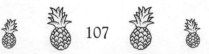

"I couldn't have done it without Mia and Charlotte," Ruby said. "They helped out in the café so I could bake a cake."

Ruby's parents beckoned her over so they could take photos.

"It was really kind of you to help Ruby," Sylvie told the girls.

"That's just what Secret Princesses do," said Charlotte. "We were trying to grant Ruby's wish of winning the Bake Off."

Sylvie looked amused. "Well, her cake was delicious."

"As delicious as the cakes you make at Wishing Star Palace?" asked Mia.

"The ones that magically change flavour?" said Charlotte.

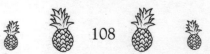

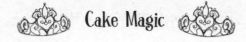
"A cake that can magically change flavour sounds amazing," Sylvie said, smiling. "I wish I could try one!"

Sylvie's cupcake-shaped pendant started to glow. There was a flash of light, and suddenly Princess Cara appeared, holding a cake shaped like Wishing Star Palace! It had thick white frosting and pink icing roses. The four turrets were tiled with white chocolate buttons and the doors and windows had sparkling jelly sweets around them.

Sylvie stared at Cara in shock. "Where did you come from?"

"Wishing Star Palace," said Cara. "I know that what the girls are telling you is hard to

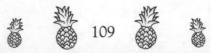

believe, but I promise you it's true."

"Try the cake," Mia urged Sylvie.

Sylvie helped herself to a slice of cake and cautiously took a bite. "It's really chocolatey," she said. As she chewed, a thoughtful look crossed her face.

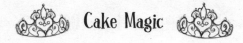 

"Or is it lemon?" Swallowing, she said, "Now it tastes like coffee cake." She took another bite and her eyes lit up. "Strawberry – my favourite!"

"What do you think?" Cara asked her.

"There's no way you could make a cake like this without using magic," Sylvie said. She brushed some crumbs off her dress. "I don't understand what the girls have been trying to tell me, but it must be true."

"It will all make sense soon," Cara assured her. "You just need to come back to Wishing Star Palace with me."

"Please go with Cara," begged Mia. "It's the only way to remember that you're a Secret Princess."

"OK," said Sylvie, nodding.

"There's something I need to do first," said Cara. She touched her wand to Mia's necklace, and then to Charlotte's. Now two blue sapphires sparkled in their half-heart pendants.

"We're halfway to earning our rings now," Charlotte said to Mia, gazing at their new jewels with pride.

"And Sylvie believes in magic again," said Mia. "So Princess Poison's curse will soon be broken."

"Before I take Sylvie back to the palace, I need to send you home," Cara told them.

"We just need to say goodbye to Ruby," said Charlotte.

The girls hurried over to their friend.

"Do you want to come back to the café with us?" Ruby asked them. "Grandma's feeling so much better that she might even do some baking!"

"That sounds great," said Mia. "But we have to go."

"Thank you for making my wish come true," Ruby said, hugging them. "I'll never forget you."

Waving goodbye to Frank and the rest of Ruby's family, Mia and Charlotte returned to Cara and Sylvie.

"We're ready to go," Charlotte told Cara. She squeezed Mia's hand. "But we'll see each other soon."

Mia smiled at her. "To grant another wish – and get another sapphire!"

Cara waved her wand and Charlotte felt magical light swirl around her, sweeping her away from the tent.

A moment later, she was back at the farmers' market.

"Charlotte!" she heard her mother calling.

"Here I am!" she said, stepping out from behind crates of fruit.

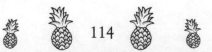

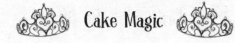 

"Did you find anything interesting?" said her dad.

Charlotte held up a prickly fruit. "Can we get a pineapple?" she asked her parents. "I can make a pineapple upside-down cake for dessert."

"That sounds lovely," said her mum. "Do you know how?"

"Yup," said Charlotte, grinning. "The secret is to use fresh pineapple – and to bake it with love!"

# The End

Join Charlotte and Mia in their next Secret Princesses adventure

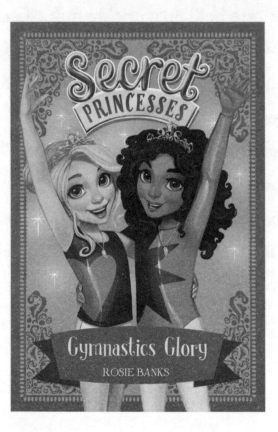

Read on for a sneak peek!

# Gymnastics Glory

"Woo hoo!" cried Mia Thompson, bending her knees and leaping up in the air.

"Higher! Higher!" shrieked her little sister, Elsie.

Mia and Elsie were jumping on the new trampoline in their back garden. It had been a present for Elsie's birthday and the two girls loved bouncing on it together.

*BOING! BOING!* Mia's long blonde hair flew up in the air as she bounced up and down on the trampoline's springy surface.

"Yippee!" cried Mia as she jumped up, kicking her legs out wide.

Elsie copied her and then they both flopped down on the trampoline, giggling and out of breath.

"Can you do a flip?" Elsie asked Mia as they lay on their backs, trying to catch their breath.

Mia shook her head. "Too bad Charlotte doesn't live here any more," she said. "She'd know how to do all sorts of tricks."

Charlotte Williams was Mia's best friend, who had moved to California not long ago. Unlike Mia, who liked baking and doing crafts, Charlotte was very sporty. Even though the girls were total opposites, they had been the closest of friends ever since they were tiny.

Mia scrambled to her feet and pulled Elsie up too. "Come on," she told her sister. "Let's bounce again!"

Mia sprang up high enough to see over the fence into her neighbours' garden, with its neatly trimmed grass and tidy flower beds. Mia grinned. It was hard to believe that someone famous had once lived there!

The next-door neighbours had a daughter called Alice, who used to babysit Mia and Charlotte. But then Alice had won a TV talent competition and became a famous pop star. Now she travelled around the world giving concerts, but her parents still lived next door to Mia.

Thanks to Alice, Mia and Charlotte were still as close as ever even though they now lived very far apart. Because Alice wasn't just a pop star, she was also a Secret Princess – someone who granted wishes using magic. Even more excitingly, she thought that Mia and Charlotte had the potential to be Secret Princesses too!

Alice had given the girls matching necklaces that allowed them to meet at an enchanted place called Wishing Star Palace. As part of their training, the girls went on amazing adventures together, helping people with magic.

As she bounced on the trampoline, Mia

wondered when she and Charlotte would get to do magic together next.

"Help!" cried Elsie, snapping Mia out of her daydream.

Elsie was trying to do a forward roll but she'd got stuck. Her head was on the trampoline and her bottom was in the air.

Read Gymnastics
Glory to find out
what happens next!

# Ruby's Pineapple Upside-Down Cake

This award-winning cake is delicious and so fun to make! Ruby always uses fresh pineapple, but tinned pineapple tastes nice too.

## Ingredients (serves 6)

For the topping:
- 50g softened butter
- 50g soft light brown sugar
- 7 pineapple rings
- Glacé cherries

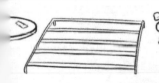

## For the cake:
- 100g softened butter
- 100g golden caster sugar
- 100g self-raising flour
- 1 tsp baking powder
- 1 tsp vanilla extract
- 2 tsp pineapple syrup/juice
- 2 eggs

## Steps

1) Get an adult to preheat the oven to 180°C/Gas Mark 4.
2) For the topping, beat the butter and sugar together until creamy and spread over the base and halfway up the sides of a round cake tin.
3) Arrange the pineapple rings on top, with the cherries in the middle of the rings.
4) Whisk all the cake ingredients together in a bowl until soft.
5) Spoon the mixture into the tin and smooth it out.
6) Bake for 35 minutes.
7) When cool, turn the cake out of the tin so that the pineapple is on the top. Enjoy!

## Princess Sylvie's Top Baking Tips

- Always ask an adult before you start baking
- Wash your hands before you begin and wear an apron to keep your clothes tidy
- Read the whole recipe through before you begin
- Weigh all your ingredients carefully
- Take your time doing each step
- Be very careful when using the oven and ask an adult to help you
- Let your cakes cool completely before eating them
- Be creative when decorating your cakes – use different colours of icing, and put sweets on top!
- Always wash up after you've finished baking

# WIN A PRINCESS GOODY BAG

*What would you wish for?*

Design your own dress and win a Secret Princesses goody bag for you and your best friend!

Charlotte and Mia get to wear beautiful dresses at Wishing Star Palace, but now they want you to design one for them.

To enter all you have to do is follow these steps:

Go to **www.secretprincessesbooks.co.uk**

♥ Click the competition module
♥ Download and print the activity sheet
♥ Design a beautiful dress for Charlotte or Mia
♥ Send your entry to:

Secret Princesses: The Sapphire Collection Competition
Hachette Children's Group
Carmelite House
50 Victoria Embankment
London
EC4Y 0DZ

Closing date: 2nd December 2017

For full terms and conditions,
www.hachettechildrens.co.uk/
TermsandConditions/secretprincessesdresscompetition.page

## Good luck!

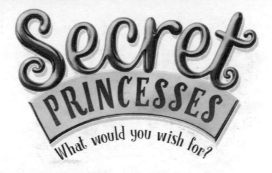

# Secret PRINCESSES

### What would you wish for?

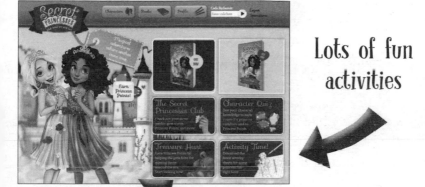

Lots of fun activities

Monthly treasure hunt

Create a secret profile

Earn princess points

Join in the fun at secretprincessesbooks.com

# Secret
## PRINCESSES

*What would you wish for?*

Are you a Secret Princess?

Join the Secret Princesses Club at:

**secretprincessesbooks.co.uk**

Explore the magic of the
Secret Princesses and discover:

❤ Special competitions! ❤
❤ Exclusive content! ❤
❤ All the latest princess news! ❤

Open to UK and Republic of Ireland residents only
Please ask your parent/guardian for their permission to join

For full terms and conditions go to
secretprincessesbooks.co.uk/terms

## Sapphire12

Enter the special code above on the website to receive

## 50 Princess Points